Resilient.
Strength.
Unconditional Love.

A Mother's Heart

Anthology Volume 3

"Through every challenge and triumph, a mother's love remains unshakable—her strength, resilience, and endless devotion make her the true definition of unconditional love."

Presented by
Theresa Jordan & 7 Phenomenal Authors

TRIUMPHANT MAGAZINE PUBLISHING

Orlando, Florida

Dedication

A Mother's Heart is a compilation that showcases the talents of seven phenomenal authors. This book is dedicated to men and women worldwide, honoring mothers from the past, present, and future. We express our gratitude for your resilience, strength, and unwavering love.

We celebrate you for the countless times you've solved problems, and held everything together, and how you transformed so many lives. Your efforts are truly valued! Your significant contributions will always be recognized and cherished.

"*But Jesus beheld them, and said unto them, With men this is impossible; but with God all things are possible.*"

Matthew 19:26

A Mother's Heart Anthology Volume 3

Proverbs 31:28-29

"Her children arise up, and call her blessed; her husband also, and he praiseth her.

Many daughters have done virtuously, but thou excellest them all. "

A Mother's Heart
is Everything

Unbreakable

Not merely a fleeting moment on the page,
Not just an annual parade—
But with each dawn and dusk that breaks,
Your love appears, authentic and unadorned.

In subtle ways unseen by the world,
You cultivate your legacy with poise.
No crown, no cape, yet you rise above,
A true hero in the eyes of your children.

You bear burdens that go unnoticed,
With calm hands and quiet strength,
Transforming chaos into solace,
And turning heavy hearts into beams of light.

Your wisdom isn't loud or boastful,
It's woven through lunches, hugs, and prayers—
A multitude of actions that may go unnoticed,
Yet God and your children feel your presence there.

This is not limited to just a single day;
This love cannot be contained within such boundaries.
You embody every season and each hour—
And every heartbeat calls out your name.
Thank you for being Unbreakable.

A Daily Prayer for Mothers

Dear Heavenly Father,

Thank You for the gift of mothers—
for their quiet strength, unwavering faith,
and the love they pour out without measure.

Bless the mother who rises early,
who gives without asking,
who carries both the weight of her family
and the light that keeps them going.

Surround her with peace when she feels unseen,
renew her strength when she is weary,
and remind her daily you see her works.

May she feel celebrated not only on special days,
but in the quiet,
in the chaos,
in the ordinary moments where her love shines
the brightest.

In Jesus' name, Amen.

"A Mother's Heart Anthology" Volume 3 was edited By Valerie Whitney

About the Editor

Valerie J. Whitney was born and raised in Norfolk, Va., the eldest of three. After graduating from high school, she enrolled in Lincoln University in Pennsylvania and graduated with a bachelor's degree in history. Afterward, she earned a master's degree in journalism from the University of Maryland in College Park.

Following graduate school, she relocated to Florida to work as a journalist. She spent four years at The Lakeland Ledger before moving to Daytona Beach, where she worked for two years as an instructor for Bethune-Cookman College.

Whitney went back into the field and spent 20 years as a reporter for The Daytona Beach News-Journal. In 2012, she returned to the classroom at Bethune-Cookman University, where she teaches journalism classes and is the adviser for the Voice of the Wildcats student newspaper and McLeod feature magazine.

She is married and the mother of a son and a daughter that both hold degrees from Lincoln, the nation's first HBCU.

Whitney had edited a cookbook titled “Good Eats” for her church, Allen Chapel A.M.E. in Daytona Beach. She published a family history titled “The Ancestors and Descendants of Grant Ulysses Garris and Mattie Gertrude Price Garris” in 2019. She is currently working on a second volume.

She likes theater, traveling, photography and reading. She is a lifetime member of the National Council of Negro Women Inc. and subscribing life member of the Alumni Association of Lincoln University. She also is a member of Alpha Kappa Alpha Sorority Inc., the National Association of Black Journalists, the Central Florida Association of Black Journalists, the East Volusia Chapter of the Afro-American Historical and Genealogy Society, as well as Roots Revisited Book Club.

For more information Professor Valerie Whitney, please email missspisces7t6@gmail.com.

ries, and experiences, including any claims of infringement of intellectual property rights or violation of privacy rights.

ISBN: 9798990403512 Softcover

Printed in the United States of America

Published by
Triumphant Magazine Publishing
P. O. Box 988
Osteen, Florida 32764

Triumphantmagazinepublishing@gmail.com or
amothersheart2023@gmail.com.

CONTENTS

A Mother's Heart Anthology Volume 3

"Mothers hold their children's hands for a short while, but their hearts forever."

Unknown

Chapter 1

The Power of Four

By Eldress Theresa Jordan

My Lovely Nana, Fannie Mims, was an entrepreneur, remarkable, and sophisticated woman indeed. She was very persistent, and she would not accept the answers "no and can't." My Nana reminded me of a woman full of determination and she would remain unstoppable until the Lord called her home.

My Nana had five grown children, and she decided to put me under her wings as her sixth child. We left New Jersey in the early '80s to start all over again in Georgia, which would create a new beginning for the two of us. When we moved to Jesup, Georgia, I was in the 8th grade. She made it clear on several occasions that she valued education. "Theresa, you are going to college, and finishing is non-negotiable," she would say.

Once I entered the 10th grade, we begin looking for assistance with financial aid because the FAFSA form needed to be completed. We had a neighbor around the corner from us that recently sent his seven children to college; however, he was unwilling to assist the two of us with guidance on how to fill out the paperwork.

My uncles, aunts, and mother hadn't attended college, so "I didn't honestly see myself attending college, but my Nana saw something inside of me that I did not see in myself." This is where her determination and unstoppable ability kicked in, and she used not receiving assistance as ammunition to get the job done. She also showed me when Jesus says, "Yes, nobody can say, No." Another valuable lesson I learned through her not giving up is that "If God is For You, Who Could Be Against Us." Once I finished college at Bethune-Cookman University, formerly known as Bethune-Cookman College, the trajectory changed for me and my family. It shifted and now we have bachelor's and master's degrees in our family, so I am happy to say, "The Lord allowed me to be the first in my family to break generational curses because He made the impossible, possible in my life.

My Nana taught me I could accomplish anything, and I could become anybody I desired to be without seeking people's validation to make it happen. She also taught me to not complain, and her favorite song was "I Won't Complain" by the Rev. Paul Jones. Also, she wanted me to remember "The Lord Will Make A Way Somehow."

On January 28, 2022, the Lord called my Nana home on my birthday. I felt this was her way of letting me know she had carried our family for 88 years, and now it is my turn to take care of the rest. We had a conversation on June 6, 2021, which was on her 88th birthday, and she wanted me to promise her that I wouldn't allow her name or the fact that she was here on this earth to be forgotten.

Well, my lovely Nana, I have kept my promise and I can't thank the Lord or you enough for bringing out the best in me. I wouldn't be the remarkable woman I am today without you.

My Aunt Dora

Loretta King aka Aunt Dora raised me like her own child and there was absolutely nothing she wouldn't do for me. She wasn't only an aunt, but a mother to me. She did everything in her power to keep our family together, and she often thought of ways to make people feel happy, appreciated, and loved. I've watched my aunt's thoughtfulness and kindness toward others throughout the years.

I learned there are givers and takers. Webster defines a giver as a person who consistently gives something to others; on the other hand, takers don't mind taking all the time. If you are a taker, please remember givers like to be appreciated too, especially during birthdays, holidays, Mother's Day, or simply just because.

Givers also don't mind receiving a phone call instead of a text message to say, "How are you doing?" or "Can I do something special for you today?"

My aunt's favorite scripture was Psalm 23, and she loved the following songs "At the Cross," and "My Soul is Anchored," by Douglas Miller.

Aunt Dora trusted in the Lord and often proved to people through her actions, "God said it, I believe it, and that settles it." We had several priceless conversations with each other, and she mentioned she wrote fifteen things down years ago that had come to pass in her life, according to Habakkuk 2:2-3. She was a woman of faith, and she knew God would answer her prayer requests because He is a Promise Keeper.

Christmas time was extra special for everyone, and I don't know about your family, but my family loved putting gifts together in the wrong boxes to make you think you were getting a certain item displayed on the outside of the box. For instance, the women in our family loved White Diamonds perfume by Elizabeth Taylor and inside the box, there wouldn't be any perfume at all, but you would find socks, towels, or washcloths. Our Christmas celebrations became more spectacular because of the surprises.

My aunt also taught me how to give myself and my friends flowers, and she kept me up to date on the latest technology. Now, she has passed that responsibility down to Dion Taylor.

Aunt Dora, I am grateful for everything you deposited into me. Thank you for the countless times you brought out the best in me. Thank you for accepting me as your own.

My Precious Granny

My great-grandmother Lucille Cudger lived in Jesup and she used to be a First Lady at Emory Chapel Methodist Church. My great-grandfather John was a pastor, and I never had an opportunity to meet him because he passed in 1965. Someone blessed my Daddy John with a Bible, and I inherited it from my granny or Nana. The Bible remains with me today, and it is significant to me because it belonged to my great-grandfather.

When I moved to Georgia, the older folks would say, "She's smelling herself or he's smelling himself," meaning the child is rebellious, strong-headed, or a little too assertive. My granny requested that I do something for her, and I can't remember what it was even today. But looking back now, I must have lost my mind for a couple of minutes because I knew better. I can't believe I had the audacity to talk back.

But when my Nana came home, she immediately went into action and grabbed me. She said, "I know you were not talking sassy to my mother."

Granny never had a problem with me again, and she became my best friend. I was like Granny, "Do you want me to go to the store to pick up some Orange Slices, moon pies, and soda to drink? Whatever you need granny, I am here for you." One day, I applied for a summer internship at a company called Rayonier in Jesup where my Aunt Dora worked. Since she consider me to be one of her children, I technically was eligible to work there. However, a gentleman that was part of the hiring committee decided he wasn't going to hire me. It was during this time my granny handed me my great-grandfather's Bible and she taught me to read, pray, and believe in God's Word. Psalm 34:6 states, "*This poor man cried, and the LORD heard him, and saved him out of all his troubles.*"

I witnessed firsthand how God turned that thing around for me. I received a phone call the next day from someone at Rayonier. The caller said, "Theresa, you can come into our office to sign your paperwork for the summer program that was designed for college students, especially for our employee's dependents." It was through my Aunt Dora and God's divine favor and blessings.

Granny, I thank you for providing me with the most precious and valuable tools in my life today, and that is prayer and relying on God's Word.

"Thy word is a lamp unto my feet, and light unto my path."

Psalm 119:105

My Mother Eloise Wade

There is only one Eloise Wade, and you are irreplaceable. I miss your laughter, prayers, songs, and daily words of encouragement. Thank you for allowing me to move to Georgia with my Nana, Granny, and Aunt Dora. I believe deep down that The Great Almighty and you knew it would propel me into my purpose and destiny in life.

Mom, you are responsible for teaching me how to celebrate life, and how not to take anything or anyone for granted. I have witnessed you speak several things into existence, which is evidence that there is power in our tongues. I am part of the Women of Worth Global Ministries founded by Dr. Katrina Ferguson, and she often reminds us daily to keep speaking until we see what we are speaking.

Mom, you have always possessed gigantic faith and I thank you for passing that down to me. The Bible says in Matthew 17:20, *"And Jesus said unto them, because of your unbelief: for verily I say unto you, If ye have fa-*

ith as a grain of mustard seed, ye shall say unto this mountain, Remove hence to yonder place; and it shall remove, and nothing shall be impossible unto you."

You were a resilient woman and an overcomer, and I am grateful the Lord chose you to be my mother.

About the Publisher

Theresa Jordan

Media Mogul. Eldress. Author.

Theresa Jordan is the CEO and Founder of Triumphant Magazine Publishing. She is the visionary behind the anthologies A Mother's Heart I, II, and III, with A Father's Heart I set to debut June 2025. Theresa, a best-selling co-author in Melanie Bonita's Daily Dose Series, was named one of the "Women in Business Who Thrive in 2025." She is delighted about her feature on a Times Square billboard for International Women's Day. On December 15, 2025, she was elevated from Minister to Eldress Jordan.

Theresa received an award from She Leads Florida on May 17, 2025. Additionally, she will receive a Lifetime Presidential Award from Black Women Who Want More (BWWWM), founded by Dr. Renee Street-Toppin, on October 11, 2025.

She feels blessed to take on empowering roles in the lives of women and youth. God has allowed her to be a part of The Women of Worth Ministries Global, leading prayer for "Winning Wednesdays" for over six years. Through her dedication and faithfulness, God inspired her to create a women's prayer group named Triumphant Women Pray

(T.W.P.), which began on Tuesday, January 21, 2025. In addition, she founded "She Poured into Me, and Now I Rise." Theresa is happily married to Daniel Jordan and is devoted to serving the Lord for the rest of her life.

FAVORITE BIBLE VERSE "But Jesus beheld them, and said unto them, With men this is impossible, but with God all things are possible." Matthew 19:26

FAVORITE QUOTES "Don't leave your potentials untouched! You plan to rob the world of it treasures if you decide to die with potentials unleashed!"

— **Dr. Myles Munroe**

"Whether you think you can, or you think you can't – you're right,"

— **Henry Ford**

For more information about Theresa Jordan, please email triumphantmagazine2017@gmail.com.

A MOTHER'S HEART VOLUME 3 - CHAPTER 1

Theresa Jordan

Photo Credit:

Anointed Visions Photography located in Deltona, Florida.

A Mother's Heart
is Everything

Psalm 139:13-14

"For thou hast possessed my reins: thou hast covered me in my mother's womb. I will praise thee; for I am fearfully and wonderfully made: marvellous are thy works; and that my soul knoweth right well."

Chapter 2

A Mother's Heart: The Legacy of Elizabeth Bethune

By Dr. Evelyn Bethune

Proverbs 31:26 (ESV) *"She opens her mouth with wisdom, and the teaching of kindness is on her tongue."*

To speak of my mother, Elizabeth Flossie Bethune, is to speak of a woman whose very existence was a living testament to faith, wisdom, and boundless love. She was not just a mother to her children; she was a mother to a community, a safe haven for the weary, a teacher of kindness, and a warrior of faith. My mother's heart was her greatest gift, and through it, she shaped the lives of so many, leaving a legacy that still ripples through time.

Elizabeth's wisdom was not merely spoken—it was lived. She carried herself with a quiet strength that demanded respect without ever needing to raise her voice. She was a woman of grace and dignity, her presence both comforting and commanding. Whether behind the chair in her beauty salon, preparing meals in our home, or offering counsel to those in need, she imparted wisdom with a gentleness that left an imprint on all who encountered her. Like the Proverbs 31 woman, she understood that wisdom was more than knowledge—it was the ability to see beyond what was, to what could be.

Though our home was not filled with extravagant riches, it overflowed with abundance—abundance of love, faith, and laughter. My mother had an uncanny ability to stretch whatever was available and create something extraordinary. A simple meal became a feast. A tired heart found renewal in her presence. A problem that seemed insurmountable found resolution through her unwavering faith in God's provision. She taught us that abundance was never about what you had in your hands but what you carried in your heart.

Mommy was a woman of many talents, a master of reinvention, a strategist before the term was popular. She was a cosmetologist, but more than that, she was an artist, sculpting beauty from the inside out. She could take thinning hair and restore confidence, not just with skillful hands but with words of encouragement that reminded people of their worth. She was an activist, ensuring that every person she encountered knew they had value, advocating for those who could not speak for themselves. She was a seamstress, a music lover, a nurturer, a disciplinarian, and a safe place all at once.

One of my mother's greatest strengths was her unwavering faith. She believed in prayer the way some believe in breathing—it was not an option; it was a necessity. I can still hear the soft hum of her prayers at night, whispered declarations of trust in God, even in the midst of hardship. She never let circumstances dictate her belief in God's promises. When money was scarce, she prayed. When life became overwhelming, she prayed. When she prayed, she that belief transformed our home into a sanctuary of faith, where miracles were not just possible but expected.

Her love was not just a feeling—it was an action. It was in the meals she cooked, the hands she held, the advice she gave, and the way she made room for anyone who needed a place to belong. She and my father, Albert, had an open-door policy before the term was ever coined. Students from Bethune-Cookman College found shelter at our home. Friends who had nowhere else to turn knew they would not be turned away. She gave freely, not out of excess but out of the understanding that giving is the true measure of wealth.

As a mother, she was both gentle and firm. She held high expectations for her children—not because she was demanding, but because she saw in us what we had not yet seen in ourselves. She expected excellence, and she instilled in us the belief that we were capable of achieving it. Education was non-negotiable. Manners were required. Accountability was expected.

And above all, faith was essential. She did not merely tell us to trust in God—she modeled it, day in and day out.

Looking back, I see how much of who I am today is because of who she was. She taught me resilience in the face of adversity, grace in the midst of struggle, and joy in the simple moments. She showed me that a mother's heart is not just about nurturing children—it is about nurturing dreams, hope, and faith in all who cross her path.

Even now, as I reflect on her legacy, I feel the warmth of her love surrounding me. Though she is no longer here in body, her spirit lingers in every lesson she taught, in every prayer she whispered, and in every life she touched.

Mommy, your heart was a reflection of God's love on this earth. Your wisdom was a beacon, your kindness a healing balm, and your faith a testament to the power of a life surrendered to God. You did not just live—you poured yourself out for others, leaving behind a legacy that will never fade.

Your love was abundant, your faith unshakable, and your heart triumphant. And for that, I will always be grateful.

Rest well, my beautiful mother. Your legacy of wisdom and kindness lives on.

Mommy, Elizabeth Sterricks Bethune.

About the Author
Dr. Evelyn Bethune

DR. EVELYN BETHUNE: A LEGACY OF LEADERSHIP, EMPOWERMENT, AND FAITH

Dr. Evelyn Bethune, the granddaughter of civil rights icon Dr. Mary McLeod Bethune, is a trailblazer in education, business, and community empowerment. With over 40 years of experience, she has dedicated her life to ensuring that African Americans, particularly women, recognize their inherent greatness and ability to shape their future.

A graduate of Bethune-Cookman University and the University of Florida, Dr. Bethune has built a multi-faceted career spanning corporate finance, entrepreneurship, media, and authorship. She has worked as an IBM budget analyst, financial planner, commodities broker, and business owner. Her expertise extends to marketing, public relations, and content creation, making her a sought-after speaker, mentor, and strategist. Her favorite things to do are singing and sewing cultural creations.

As the founder of **History in the Making Coaching Network, Inc.**, Dr. Bethune helps individuals tap into their ancestral wisdom and personal strengths to achieve success. Her programs, such as the masterclass *Greatness is In Your DNA,* focus on faith, leadership, and economic empowerment. She is also a co-creator of **Billionaire Bot Chics**, an initiative that helps Black women entrepreneurs leverage AI and technology to build wealth while maintaining their spiritual values.

Dr. Bethune is a passionate author whose works include *Bethune: Out of Darkness into the Light of Freedom* and *The Bethune Blueprint: Transforming Your Life Through the Lessons of Dr. Mary McLeod Bethune*. Through her books, she preserves the legacy of her grandmother while inspiring future generations to embrace resilience and purpose. The Bethune Publishing House, Inc. is one of the successful business projects in which she participates.

Committed to service, Dr. Bethune is a **Life Member of the National Council of Negro Women (NCNW), a member of the Association for the Study of African Life and History, (ASALH), the NAACP, and Bethune-Cookman University Alumni Association**. She is active in the **African Methodist Episcopal Church**, supporting the Women's Missionary Society, YPD Youth Program, and Restoration House for the homeless.

Her groundbreaking achievements include being the **first African American woman to own a race car in the NASCAR Subway Jalapeno 250 in 2011 at Daytona International Speedway**.

Dr. Evelyn Bethune continues to be a beacon of faith, leadership, and empowerment, using her platform to uplift and transform lives, ensuring that the legacy of strength and excellence in the Black community endures for generations to come.

For more information about Dr. Evelyn Bethune, please email dreveIyn@greatnessdna.com.

A MOTHER'S HEART VOLUME 3 - CHAPTER 2

Dr. Evelyn Bethune

A Mother's Heart
is Everything

Chapter 3

Everyday Princess: Evangelist Janie Brinson

By Vivaloria Brinson

In Sir Earl Spencer's oration, he remarked of the late Princess Diana:

"No Need for Royal Title"

"Diana was the very essence of compassion, of duty, of style, of beauty. All over the world she was a symbol of selfless humanity. Someone with a natural nobility who was classless and who proved in the last year that she needed no royal title to continue to generate her particular brand of magic.

In Queen Elizabeth II's tribute to Diana on September 9, 1997, she said, "She (Diana) was an exceptional and gifted human being. In good times and bad, she never lost her capacity to smile and laugh, nor to inspire others with her warmth and kindness. I admired and respected her -- for her energy and commitment to others, and especially for her devotion to her two boys."

Diana was hailed as "the People's Princess."

When one speaks of a mother's heart, one can't help to think of a person whose lifestyle is that of grace and generosity. A person who doesn't seek out a platform for all to see, but performs good works to all she sees. A person whose words of wisdom and simple acts of kindness makes a tremendous, profound impact on those she comes into contact with. A person whose strives to improve the lives of others even if it means a personal sacrifice.

Having never met Princess Diana, what I knew of her was through the eyes of the media, which can sometimes be skewed or bias. I saw clips of her visiting the orphanage. I saw pictures of her being personable with the commoners. There would be videos posted of her delicately navigating her two children through the perils of always being public figures. I can't speak to the every-day life of Princess Diana, but I can personally attest to what I see from day to day in the life of my mom with no angles and no filters.

Proverbs 31 describes a virtuous woman who is strong, wise, and compassionate. My mom is the epitome of that kind of woman. She didn't come from an affluent family yet her family was influential in the manner in which her grandmother and mother cared for their family plus the neighborhood children. Like a good student, my mom took what she saw and applied it. What woman would work a full-time job and leave that job to report to her next duty of being the leading lady i.e. Pastor's wife that included everything from singing in the choir, teaching Sunday School, visiting members and non-members, and the like? What kind of woman would open her home to those in transition sometimes without an explanation or planning? What kind of a woman would go out to shop for herself but ends up purchasing items for everyone else but herself? What kind of woman calls you out of the blue and say "come by and get your package?" Have you ever met a woman who possesses natural and spiritual intuition that is able to see what is sometimes not readily visible or hear what may not come audibly out of your mouth? Have you seen her? Tell me, have you seen her?

To answer all these questions, I have the answer; her name is Janie Brinson. I'm a witness to how my mom, after retiring from her first career, rose early to return back to school and pursue her degree. I saw her sit in the inclement weather to the very end to cheer my brother on as his pee-wee football team is down in the score 40-to-0, holding on to a glimmer of hope that they would get on the scoreboard. By the way, the team did not score but my mom celebrated my brother as if they walked away with the win. She also gave me and his other siblings the lecture on how important it is to not abandon the cause because it does not look good--stick it out. I currently see my mom push pass challenges to care for my grandmother in her twilight years and she does so with an attitude of willingness to serve.

Although many say that they don't make those kinds of women anymore, I can refute that because my mom is a prototype that my sisters and I are patterning after. She does not possess an auspicious title. She does not require the accolades of the paparazzi. What she does possess is Godly Character which empowers her to stand tall despite her 5'2' frame and excel many.

Today, I hail my mom -Janie Brinson- as the "Everyday Princess" who is the same in the lows of life as she is in the highs of life.

A MOTHER'S HEART VOLUME 3 - CHAPTER 3

My Mom, Janie Brinson.

About the Author

Vivaloria Brinson

Vivaloria Brinson is an educator within the Orange County Public School system, fulfilling various roles throughout her career. She graduated from Florida State University with a Bachelors of Science degree in Psychology (Major)/Sociology (Minor). After graduation, she returned to her hometown to serve alongside her parents, Bishop Norris and Evangelist Janie Brinson, in ministry.

In addition to being an educator, she is the Lead Pastor of Hart Temple in DeLand, Florida. Her daily pursuit is to successfully assist others with the available resources at her disposal. Inspired by the song "If I Can Help Somebody," her passion comes from the following lines:

If I can help somebody, as I pass along,
If I can cheer somebody, with a word or song…
Then my living shall not be in vain.
If I can do my duty, as a good man ought…
Then my living shall not be in vain.

A MOTHER'S HEART VOLUME 3 - CHAPTER 3

Vivaloria Brinson

A Mother's Heart
is Everything

Chapter 4

And She Wears the Title Well, the Dr. Kay Williams-Dawson Motherhood Story

By Bishop Melvin C. Dawson, Jr.

If ever there was a mandating need to drop the terminology known as "Stepmom," it is with my wife, Dr. Kay Williams-Dawson. Due to her overcoming battle with cancer, during her college days at Sam Houston State University (Houston, TX), Kay was not able to have children of her own. But unless you know the story, you would never know it by her interactions with our children, Aryelle, Melvin III, Ahkeem, and Joseph…….and our granddaughter, Tamia.

After the failure of my first marriage (and I will be the first to admit, it was all my fault), God gave me another chance to correct my initial faults. In the words of the singer Larry Graham, she became my "One In A Million," and echoing the words of Luther Vandross, my "Forever, For Always, For Love." Many often wonder what makes a woman become a great mother, especially when there are so many horror stories of children growing up scared and abused by the lack of love and affection needed from their mother. I believe the secret to Kay's success is threefold, if you will allow me to share:

"A Reflection of Her Mother's Love and Affection"

Dr. Kay has this familiar line that she always uses to boast on her beauty, when she says, "I LOOK GOOD BECAUSE MY MOMMA LOOKS GOOD!" But it's not just the looks. Her mom, Margaret Williams, affectionately known by many as "Lady" or "Dear," is a retired educator and devoted Christian woman, who has served in the church all of her life. When you see the bond that Kay and her mom have, then you know how she is able to bond with our children (who all happen to be grown and in their thirties). Her mother, Lady Margaret, was not just a great mother to her children, Anita Kay and Lyndon Keith, but if you were to travel through the small towns of Shepherd, TX (where Kay was born and raised), and Greenville, TX (where Lady Margaret was born and raised), you will run into a number of adults and youth alike, who feel as if she has mothered and nurtured them throughout their lifetime. Of a certain, Lady Margaret held true to the words of King Solomon, as recorded in Proverbs 22:6,

"Train up a child in the way he should go: And when he is old, he will not depart from it."

She did, indeed, train Kay up correctly, and all of her wonderful motherly qualities of nurturing and caring not only rubbed off onto Kay, but has been embedded into her soul.

Lady Margaret and My Wife, Dr. Kay Williams-Dawson.

A MOTHER'S HEART VOLUME 3 - CHAPTER 4

"An Understood Responsibility of Motherhood"

Our children, like the children of the Proverbs 31 Virtuous Woman Story, rise up and call her blessed, because they know Kay understands the responsibility of motherhood. Accepting my proposal for marriage, she immediately counted up the cost of the "wonderful baggage" that was coming along with me........Aryelle, Melvin III, and Ahkeem (and we later adopted Joseph to our clan). She knew that motherhood would come at a great cost, but she was willing to pay up. And at the same time, she was putting forth a great effort to make sure her brother's daughters (Regina, Brioni, and Leah) were also going to be a viable part of our immediate family. And when I tell you, she never dropped the ball......SHE NEVER DROPPED THE BALL, even though the task was not always easy. She successfully juggled motherhood with her career, marriage, church, civic, political, and sorority duties. And, she made it look easy.

A lot of times, people are not willing to get advice from others in areas unfamiliar to them, and yet I remember times when Kay would have conversations with older Mothers of the Church, and seek wisdom to be the best at what she had chosen to be as a wife and mother. Again, this is probably a direct reflection of the relationship that she had with her own mom, Lady Margaret, and it paid off well in the long run.

"The Reality of Loving the Children Equally, but With Different Methodologies"

Probably the greatest attribute of my wife, Dr. Kay, as it relates to her being a great mother, is her ability to have the wisdom to know that she would need to extend love to our children, but (perhaps) in different ways. While our house is filled with pictures of the entire family, you will also find pictures where, in different locations and settings, it's just Kay and Aryelle........or Kay and Melvin III.......or Kay and Ahkeem.......or Kay and Joseph. Somehow, through the motherly love of careful observation, Kay knew early on in her new role as a mother, she would need to develop equal but separate relationships with each of our children. You must keep in mind that my first divorce was not easy on our children, as they would be subliminally pulled in different directions from outside forces choosing sides against their mothers. It was Kay who helped to develop a plan that would prove successful in our rearing of our children.

The plan was relatively simple, but brilliant in its design. We would give our children the opportunity to live with either parents, however, wherever they decided to stay in Elementary School, they would have to stay through the 5th grade. Should they desire to move after elementary, they would have to remain wherever they started Middle School, from 6th through 8th grade. Then if they wanted to make a change during High School, they would have to remain in that place throughout the duration of 9th-12th grade. This proved to be a wonderful idea, giving our children the comfortableness to have some say so in their own educational matriculation, and for this, our children successfully survived, what many children suffer from, victims of divorce.

Yes, when it comes to the idea of Motherhood, She Wears the Title Well.

Dr. Kay Williams-Dawson

About the Author

Bishop Melvin C. Dawson, Jr.

Bishop Melvin C. Dawson, Jr, born March 27, 1963, to the late Elder Melvin C. Dawson, Sr., and the late Evangelist Annie D. Zow Dawson.

He is proud to have been raised in the city of DeLand, FL., in which was the place of his early educational matriculation, graduating from DeLand Senior High School in 1981. He graduated with a Bachelor of Science Degree from the Bethune-Cookman University in 1985, Majoring in Psychology, and a Minor in English. In relations to his degree, he has served as a Substance Abuse Counselor, Behavior Modification Specialist (for those with Intellectual Developmental Disorders), Counselor for Emotionally Disturbed Adolescents and Kids In Distress, Christian Counseling with Special Emphasis on Marriage Enrichment and Family Bonding.

Bishop Dawson's preaching ministry has expanded over 40 years, and has blessed him to serve as the Founder and Bishop of the Cathedral of Praise Church (Miami, FL), where his wife, Dr. Kay Williams-Dawson serves as Senior Pastor. Bishop Dawson now uses his gifts and talents to serve as Director of Spiritual Development. As a Bishop of the Lord's Church, and under the affiliation of Kingdom Connection Fellowship International, he currently serves as KCFI-Florida Jurisdiction State Bishop.

Wearing many career hats, Bishop Dawson is recognized nationally and internationally as a Preacher, Teacher, Counselor, Actor, Playwright, Singer, Musician, Director, Gospel Recording Artist, and Author of several books. He is sought after by many who desire to hear him share the Proclaimed Gospel of Jesus Christ, as he has been afforded the opportunity to share the gospel throughout the U.S., Caribbean Islands, and as far as South Africa (Johannesburg and Soweto).

He is married to the lovely Dr. Kay Williams-Dawson, and has four adult children, Aryelle, Melvin III, Ahkeem, and Joseph; and one granddaughter, Tamia.

For more information about Bishop Melvin C. Dawson, Jr, please email Melvindawsonministries@yahoo.com.

Bishop Melvin C. Dawson, Jr.

A Mother's Heart is Everything

Chapter 5

Wow! Me, A Mother?

By Veronica Gomez

Wow! Me, A mother? I cannot believe it.

When I first became a mother, I could not believe how much it would change my life. I could not believe how fast my life would shift.

I gave up everything I knew to become the best mother I could be for this tiny little boy.

When we first have children, we envision "that" life: the white fence, the husband and the dogs running around in the yard. That is what we are taught and told as we grow up, as we hit the "motherhood" milestone in life.

My experience happened to be nothing of that sort. I could not believe after three miscarriages that I was finally holding this little boy in my arms. As I looked into his eyes I could see my reflection. All I could think and say was, "Wow! Me, A mother? Finally!" and "Thank You, God!"

I was convinced that motherhood was not going to be an experience for me. I was broken year after year when I lost my babies. I asked God so many times why he was putting me through this?

Why are you making me suffer?

Why are you making me feel like I am not worthy enough to be a mother?

Can you believe I really sat there and questioned God? Back slid and had the nerve to ask God why He was doing this to me?

I fell into a deep depression. I was attached to alcohol and marijuana. I became so numb to everyone and everything. I stopped caring about everything and everyone. I felt worthless, as a woman, as a partner. I was alone in this place. My family was miles away.

I pretended to be present every day even though I was hurting inside.

Then finally one day it happened.

I took a pregnancy test. I saw the result. I was happy, but because of my history, I was scared.

When I was blessed with my son, I was in one of the worst seasons of my life. I became a single mother. The illusion of raising a family depressed me for years with my son. "God, you gave me this son, and now I am raising him on my own." That is all I could think or say. I cannot believe I went through these past 12 years with someone for me to end up a single mother. I must do this alone now.

Are you kidding me God?

Eventually, I got over that "what if" moment in my life and put on my big girl pants and decided to just move forward in my life. It was just me and this cute little boy, trying to figure out life. Trying to navigate this journey with no close family nearby. I had a small group of friends at the time, but I always felt alone. After three years of trying to figure out life on my own and leaving God out of my life, I met a man named Rubin Ross. Rubin became an important part of my motherhood journey. Rubin and I worked together at Denny's. He became a mentor without me even realizing it.

One day Rubin handed me a card. It was a church card. At first glance I chuckled to myself. Rubin had no idea what I went through, or what I was going through...how my living situation was. He did not see through the mask I was wearing.

Or did he?

I grabbed the card. The following Sunday I went to the church on the card, and it was as if God was speaking directly to me. I broke down like I have never broken down before. Rubin was there smiling as I was releasing years of hurt and pain. Years of questioning why God did what he did all for this moment.

I looked back at my son who was sitting there calmly smiling, and I could not help but smile and say thank you, God.

In Proverbs 22:6 it says that we must *train a child in the way he should go.*

As mothers we put so much pressure on ourselves. We want a perfect life. We want the perfect family. We don't want to go through the trials or the storms. But, it's in those storms and trials that help mold us to become the women and mothers we are destined to become.

Wow! Me, A Mother?

Isaiah 66:13 compares *God's comfort for his people to the comfort a mother gives her child.* A mother's love is unconditional such as God's love for us. We must not forget that even in our storms.

I look back now at my full story and I thank God for sending me my angel at such a time in my life. I had thoughts of suicide right before I met him. If it were not for his kindness, his persistence, and his guidance I could have left my son motherless. (Rest in peace to my dear (mentor)

Then, at the age of 33, I became a proud mother of two children. God has been our foundation and our rock!

I realize now why God put me through what I went through as a single mother.

He was preparing me for my daughter. God knew exactly what he was doing from start to finish on my journey of motherhood.

I can proudly say at 37, I am a healed and mighty, praying Woman of God. To be able to raise my daughter as a healed woman helps break the generational curses that may have been attached to me.

I thank God for my trial's and my storms!

I thank God for molding me into the woman and mother I am today!

If it were not for the storms.

Wow! Me, A Mother.

A Mother's Heart is Everything

About the Author

Veronica Gomez

Moyi, a multi-talented international artist from Deltona, Florida, is renowned for her abilities as a rapper, singer, and songwriter.

Moyi was born on November 2, 1987. Originally from Buffalo, New York, she is described as an old soul who spreads positivity through her music, guiding those who be struggling to strengthen their faith.

Apart from her music career, Moyi is a devoted mother of two, a published author, a photographer, and a host of her very own podcast "*Moyivation,*" which focuses on motivating and encouraging her listeners.

Her music is available on all streaming platforms, and the podcast can be found on numerous platforms.

Moyi is an advocate for youth empowerment under the leadership of Pedro Rodriguez with Urban Youth Justice.

With a free-spirited personality and a focus on positivity, Moyi's presence brings peace, calmness, and joy to those around her.

For more details or to inquire about speaking engagements, please contact Bookmoyi@mail.com.

A MOTHER'S HEART VOLUME 3 - CHAPTER 5

Veronica Gomez

A Mother's Heart
is Everything

Proverbs 31:28–29

"Her children arise up, and call her blessed; her husband also, and he praises her: Many daughters have done virtuously, but thou excellest them all."

Chapter 6

Living Legacy of Miss Emma

By Leroy Joe Jr.

Emma Jean Joe was born in the late 1940s in Belle Glade, Florida. She lived in the Pahokee/Silver City area. She was the second oldest child, a brother Tommie Lee Joe preceded her in death, born to Leroy and Annie Doris Joe. Her parents are now deceased.

Emma's parents and her two siblings--Leroy and Dorothy-- left South Florida searching for a better life. They moved to Polk County, Florida, where the family settle in a rural community called Gordonville with only $300. The family was at the point of homelessness when her father found a job.

Emma attended Union Academy, which was an all-Black school in 1965, then transferred to Bartow Senior High School. She graduated in 1967 with the first Black class to graduate from Bartow Senior High School, now known as Bartow International Baccalaureate High School.

Her parents weren't financially able to send her to college, so Emma attended a practical nursing class at the Bartow Airbase at the Polk Vocational Technical Center for $75, which covered the cost of books, tuition and supplies. After graduating from the practical nursing class, Emma worked at Polk General Hospital for many years before attending Polk Community College in Winter Haven, Florida. She went on to graduate in 1982 as a registered nurse and worked at Lakeland General Hospital until 2011. Emma then began working at Bartow Rehabilitation Center until present.

Emma was always resourceful, thoughtful and compassionate. Family members knew that if there was a way to get any job done, she would come up with a way to solve most problems. And, if she couldn't solve the problem, she would find someone who could provide a solution.

Emma's passion for serving in the healthcare industry grew as the years progressed. She took her profession very serious putting herself second while caring for numerous patients in hospitals and nursing home facilities. Her nursing career has spanned over 50 years and counting. Perhaps, most importantly, is the fact that she provided care for her daughter, mother and father during their time of need. She also took on the task of hosting all the family gatherings. Again, she was very proficient at anything she put her hand to do. Likewise, she always had a heart of caring for all of God's creation from animals to nature, especially a green thumb for landscaping and gardening.

She purchased her first home in Gordon Heights, Florida, where she raised three beautiful children--daughter Erika (now deceased), son Kenneth, and daughter Cassandra. Both are alive and have families of their own. Emma has three grandchildren Natalia, Sherrell and Christian, all of whom she loves dearly.

What is legacy? Legacy is not only when someone dies and leaves money or any amount of wealth or assets but legacy is the knowledge, wisdom and understanding that has been gained from the one who passed it down. This is the life and legacy of Miss Emma and what it means to her loved ones and the world at large. Each one of us will leave some form of legacy to those who will follow us.

Presently Emma is building that legacy for those of us that are living now and in the future. Emma's interests are as diverse as her commitment to her family and community. She was well versed in anything she sets her mind to doing, she found joy engaging in conversations about her younger years traveling and experiencing the highs and lows of everyday life.

Psalm 112:2: "A good man leaves an inheritance to his children's children, And the wealth of the sinner is stored up for the righteous." **New Living Translation**.

Emma's traits—hardworking, determined, focused and may more--were gifted to her by her parents Leroy and Annie. She never complained, at least we never heard her complain. She kept on moving forward, staying focused on what was good in her sight to do, which was close to being on target!

Emma Jean Joe

Her life and legacy produced a gift that keeps on giving and it proves that hard work pays off even in the toughest of times. In her younger years she was a loyal member serving on the usher board at First Providence Missionary Baptist Church, which is the oldest African American church in Polk County.

She has always been a tireless advocate for those in need, always ready to lend a hand and make a difference in the lives of others. Emma has touched many lives. That is her legacy and we are all better for it.

About the Author

Leroy Joe Jr.

Leroy Joe Jr. was born in the small rural town of Pahokee, Florida, and raised in Bartow by his parents Leroy Joe Sr. and Annie Joe.

His parents were farm workers, but he decided to go another way and served his country by enlisting in the U.S. Army, making it a career. During his time in the army, he became proficient in his military occupation as a food service specialist. He excelled throughout the ranks and became a senior non-commissioned officer leading his team to become winners of the coveted Phillip A. Connelly Award for Excellence in Army Foodservice.

Also, while in the military, he attended several leadership academies and enrolled in college courses that would enhance his academic abilities. His career covered over 22 years.

Immediately after retirement from the military, Leroy Joe Jr. continued to serve in the community as a board member for the West Bartow Front Porch Governor's Initiative, team captain of the All-Pro Dads program, board member for the Wings of Eagles Outreach International, and as a board member for the Architectural Review board in the city of Bartow.

During the recent pandemic, he founded Humanitarian Outreach Ministries Inc 2021. Among other accomplishments, he earned an undergraduate certificate in biblical studies in 1999 from Liberty University in Lynchburg, Virginia. He also graduated with a bachelor's degree from the College of Theology in Christian Studies in 2014 from Grand Canyon University, Phoenix, Arizona.

For more information about Leroy Joe Jr., please email sfcjoe65@gmail.com.

Leroy Joe Jr.

Resilient.
Strength.
Unconditional Love.

Psalm 121:1

"I will lift up my eyes unto the hills, from whence cometh my help."

Chapter 7

A Broken-Hearted Mother - Now A Healed Mother

By Pastor Dr. Trish Redding, DD

I was born to Lamar and Mildred Redding in June 1953. My sister and I were placed in foster care by court order, transferring custody of my mother's children. There was an adoption petition for my older sister, and my older brother was taken in by my aunt and uncle from Niagara Falls.

The family interested in adopting my sister did not want to adopt me. But, the court ruled that we should not be separated. So, the couple adopted me as well.

I cannot fully understand what my mother felt during that period. Her marriage ended and she lost us, her three children. I often saw her crying, likely due to my dad. I also heard about another child with my brother's name and a mother named Mildred.

My mom was devastated and became reckless in her lifestyle. She would disappear for extended periods, only showing up on Thanksgiving, Christmas, and our birthdays for a few days before leaving again.

She was living a broken life and needed healing. Though she moved past my dad's actions, I am not sure if she ever forgave him. She often said he wanted a divorce, but she always refused and insisted on remaining a Redding.

When I was in sixth grade, I learned that the individual who filed a complaint against my mother, resulting in the removal of her children from her care, was the same person who had previously taken my mother from her own mother and had her mother declared unfit to raise a child. This situation raises questions about how one person could affect a family in such significant ways. I have found it difficult, with many relatives still in Sanford, to understand the reasons behind these events.

My grandfather told me that when my mother learned about my father's involvement with another woman, she found it difficult to think clearly. They married shortly after high school and began a family. According to my grandfather, my father caused significant emotional damage to her. He said that she would experience flashbacks during each pregnancy, leading to the state intervening and taking her baby within a few days.

My foster mother often shared distressing stories about my biological mother, alleging that she abandoned me on her doorstep and did not want me. She portrayed my mother as being unfit. I was unsure of how to interpret these narratives until I had a conversation with my grandfather. Although I could not fully understand what my mother was going through, I was acutely aware of my own pain. I desired to know more about my mother, but I was uncertain if she would accept me.

At some point, my mother turned her life around and moved from Florida to Syracuse, N.Y., where her mother lived. Pregnant with my baby sister and with my baby brother in tow, she worked at Syracuse University and bartended on weekends at the English Inn. She took in a young girl from the streets, helped her through nursing school, and they became close friends. Her two best friends were Mary Lee and Rosalee.

In 1969, my mother visited on my birthday and witnessed my foster mother using a mop handle to choke me. My mother and my foster mother had a serious disagreement. Later that day, I asked my mother if I could move to New York with her and she agreed. She explained that she had previously attempted to remove me from the foster care system but had been unsuccessful. Now that I was old enough to speak for myself, she decided to try again. This time, she succeeded.

I spent the next three years getting to know my mother and seeing her love for all her children. She regretted not being a better mother and wished she could have had all her children together. We enjoyed long walks and meaningful conversations about life. She shared her difficult past and was ashamed of it but grateful my sister and I were finally with her.

My mother was full of joy and laughter, always brightening the room. Sadness could not stay around her. She believed laughter was the best medicine. Though she never professed Christ as Lord, she would not let me disrespect God. One Easter, my girlfriend and I went to church to mock those who danced and shouted. When my mother found out, she came to the church, had us leave, and made us promise never to do that again. She taught me the importance of honoring my parents to live a long life.

My mother's close friend had a daughter who became my best friend. She introduced me to Syracuse and guided me during my teenage years. She also accompanied us on our trips to Florida when we visited my grandfather. My grandfather was delighted that we were all reunited, and I shared his sentiment.

I still reflect on how things turned out and am grateful for spending time with my mother, who found happiness and contentment in her life.

On Thanksgiving Day in 1972, my mother became ill. When we called for an ambulance to take her to the hospital, she asked me not to let them take her. The ambulance transported her to the hospital on Monday morning, and by Wednesday morning, she had passed away. She anticipated her departure, but I was unaware of it at the time. I spent the best years of my life with my mother, Mildred Elizabeth Redding.

Presenting Pastor Dr. Trish and her daughter, Matanya.

Meet Corey Mills, the grandson of Pastor Dr. Trish and her daughter, Matanya.

About the Author

Pastor Dr. Trish Redding, DD

Dr. Patricia D. Redding, affectionately known as Pastor Trish, was born in June 1953 in Sanford, Florida. She attended Hopper Elementary School and Crooms High School in Sanford before relocating to Syracuse, New York, in 1969. She completed her secondary education at Henniger High School in Syracuse, graduating in 1971. Dr. Redding commenced her higher education at Onondaga Community College in Syracuse and subsequently earned a Doctor of Divinity Degree from Joshua Generation Bible College in Orlando, Florida.

In August 1978, Dr. Redding embraced her faith at the Refuge Tabernacle Church of God in Christ in Syracuse, New York, under the leadership of Pastor Theodore McCrae.

Dr. Redding's early life began in the foster care system, where she faced significant challenges and endured considerable abuse administered as discipline. The reasons for this mistreatment were never made clear to her. She believes that God has a plan for each person and allows necessary events to fulfill his plan. Her foster parents played a crucial role in shaping her character and guiding her towards God's purpose.

She currently serves as one of the ordained associate pastors at the River of Life Christian Center in Orlando, Florida, under the leadership of Dr. Marvin and Dr. Deborah Jackson, and teaches the Senior Bible Study Group. Dr. Redding has collaborated with several pastors and congregations in her evangelistic outreach ministry, including The Macedonia Church of God in Christ (Suisun City, CA), The Friendship Baptist Church (Yorba Linda, CA), The Howell Missionary Baptist Church Norcross, GA). and Light cross, GA), and Light of The World International Church (Sarasota, FL).

Diagnosed with terminal cancer in 1992 and given six months to live, Dr. Redding relied on faith, citing Psalms 118:17, *"I will live and not die and declare the works of the Lord."* After seven years, she was declared cancer-free.

The family experienced the loss of their oldest sister on Thanksgiving Day 2023, where Dr. Redding delivered words of hope and encouragement at the homegoing service. Dr. Redding is the mother of one, Matanya, and grandmother of one, Corey Mills. She also has two feline companions, Samuel and Silas.

For more information about, Dr. Patricia D. Redding please email tredding20@gmail.com.

Pastor Dr. Trish Redding, DD

A Mother's Heart
is Everything

Proverbs 31:10

"Who can find a virtuous woman? for her price is far above rubies."

Chapter 8

She Who Sacrificed

By Betty R. Smith

Katie Lee Boyd was born April 02, 1939 to the parents of Julius Boyd and Lillian Wilson Boyd. She was the fifth of 15 children. Times were not easy with a family that large, and there were challenges, but God sustained the family through it all.

At the age of 17, she married our father, Alonzo Richardson and moving forward she always signed her name as Katie Lee Boyd Richardson.

Our mother gave birth to six children by the time she was 24. Growing up then was a lot different than it is now.

As little ones, five of us shared one bedroom, while our baby sister always slept with our Mom and Dad. We got along in that crowded bedroom and never complained because we had nothing or no one to compare living conditions with. We didn't know just how poor we were. We entertained ourselves as children by playing cowboys, and using sticks as the guns. We played hide and seek, and there was this big saw mill in the woods behind our house where we would dive in the huge pile of saw dust and tiny wood shavings.

I also remember soldiers camping in the woods behind our house and when they left, they would leave food behind like canned peanut butter, crackers, sardines and other miscellaneous items. When we saw the soldiers leaving, we would hurry and salvage what we could. To us, that experience was awesome. Even though I don't remember us being cold or hungry, I do remember my mother saying that at times as babies that we had to suck sugar water from the baby bottle because there was no milk. We thrived off her love for us, she never gave up.

Speaking with my siblings concerning our mom, we shared what we remember as children while growing up.

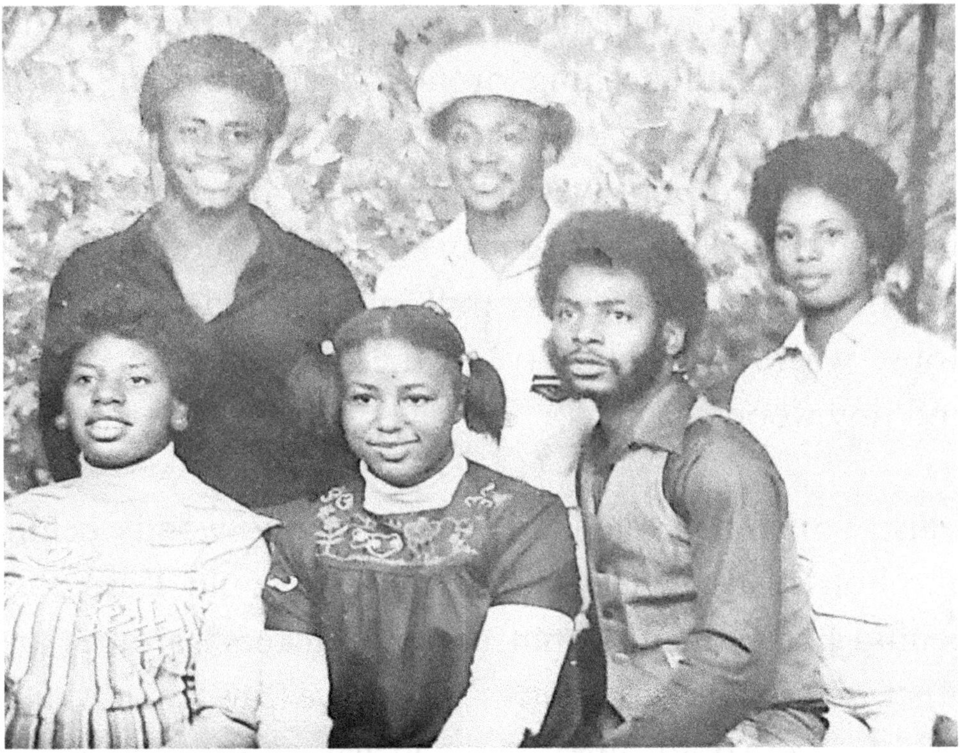

Front row, from left to right: Betty, Barbara, Jerry
Back row, from left to right: Michael, Jimmy, Lizzie

My eldest sister and the oldest child remember our mom walking to church while we stayed home. She remembers us siblings never going dirty or unkept. What little we had was clean and she used a hot comb on our hair. Our mom did other women's hair by straightening it and then using the hot marcel curlers. She would blow the hot tools that she used and had a damp cloth on standby to wipe off the excess oil from pressing the hair. We could sometimes hear the sizzling from the heat and oil combination on the hair. She was good at it too.

I remember once we had an old washing machine, the one with the two rollers on top that came together, and you would put your clothes in between the rollers to wring them out from the tub that was attached to the wringer. The tub had an agitator, and we had to manually put water in the tub for washing. The washing machine was kept on the back porch and one day when our mom was washing, I heard a scream and ran to get our dad only to find our mother's hand was caught between the rollers. Our dad quickly unplugged the machine and pried the rollers apart to release her hand. I saw him examine her hand and when all was calm, she continued washing. Sometime later my dad would take her to the launderette and she would come home and hang them out on the line.

As a child we remember our mother as being a fantastic cook. Our favorite meals were salmon patties, liver with gravy and onions, squirrel and rabbit with the best gravy in the world. She never really taught us how to cook, there was just not enough food to waste in case we messed up. However, she did buy my sister and I a sewing machine and she would take us to buy cloth and patterns from the local store. We took home economics in high school and there we learned how to sew and to cook simple stuff. Our mother never worked while we were growing up and she said she would ease a few dollars out of the grocery money that our dad gave her. She also saved green backed stamps, and she took pride in going to that store to trade her book of stamps in.

Now as you can see our mother was a very beautiful woman. She had awesome features. One of her sisters said they used to pick on her and call her the "pretty one." She was petite and took pride in her hair, nails, and skin. She was very resourceful and did not let challenges get in the way.

Our Mother, Katie Lee Boyd Richardson.

God knew exactly what He was doing when our mom, at age 24, had a child born with cerebral palsy. Barbara, our mom's last child, a girl, our beautiful sister was both mentally and physically challenged. God put her with a family who never left her or mistreated her. After hearing stories about people dropping their family members off at various institutions that became their home and the parents never looked back, not a call or visit because for them, it was too much for them to sacrifice.

We would hear conversations between our mom and dad about our sister. Mom acknowledged the situation and dad saying there was nothing wrong. Our sister was well over a year old and wasn't walking or talking and she would scoot on the floor on her bottom to get around. I can't piece together how all this happened but the next thing we as siblings knew, our baby sister came home fitted with a leg brace and it was then that she learned how to walk. I remember our mom spending countless hours walking her baby girl. We had a dirt yard and driveway, and she would walk her around in the yard, to the mailbox, in the house, just getting her used to her leg brace. When our mom felt confident that the rest of us could walk with her, she let us give it a try. It was a privilege to be able to help our sister on her new journey.

Our mom always kept our sister looking healthy and neat because we knew that people were going to stare out of ignorance. Our sister did go to public school and when she went as far as she could, she went to Piedmont Skills where the clients learned how to function in an advanced level of society. They would get small pay for their "work" and that made her feel like she was contributing to her cost of living.

Our mom never worked a real job because everything she did centered around our sister's needs. Our mother stayed with her day and night even as an adult. Occasionally our mom would go out with friends or to various other functions and that's when we were glad to step in and care for our sister. Our mother once said that she hoped that Barbara would transition before her because she felt that no one else would take care of her the way she did. Sadly, this became true. We lost Barbara in 2003 just short of her 40th birthday. She was in the hospital for a while before she passed, and the doctors and nurses told our mom that they could tell that Barbara was well taken care of. It did our mom good to hear that from someone outside of the family but especially from someone in the medical field.

We could tell that our mom missed her baby girl. She didn't quite know what to do with herself so she got a part-time job working in the kitchen at a daycare. She went to a few places and enjoyed a few things. One year later in 2004, she who sacrificed was diagnosed with a tumor and later transitioned in 2005. She left a legacy with us. The legacy of resilience and putting yourself last so that others could thrive.

Thank you, Mom.

About the Author

Betty R. Smith

Betty R. Smith is a native of South Carolina from a little town called Fountain Inn, which is about 20 miles south of Greenville. Born in 1958, she was the third of six children. She was educated in the public schools of Greenville County and later received an associate degree in materials management from Greenville Technical College.

In June of 1978, Betty married the love of her life, Curtis N. Smith, and from that union three children were born. She has worked at various corporations mainly in the quality sector as a senior quality lab technician.

Betty is now retired and is the proud grandmother of three. She loves gardening, reading for personal development, and taking intermittent saxophone lessons whenever time allows. She also loves to travel, attend musicals and visit various museums.

Spending time with family, friends and attending church are things that she enjoys, too. Betty is a Sunday School teacher for the women's class and has held several leadership roles in the body of Christ. She continues to strive to be that beacon of light to the lost, hopeless, and confused.

In December of 2023, after more than 44 years of marriage, Betty became a widow. It was totally unexpected, and she misses her husband dearly. She starts her days with prayer, knowing that it is the Lord who has and will continue to sustain her throughout her life, especially since the loss of her husband.

The Lord is the center of her life, and she dedicates each day to worshiping and praising Him. As a little girl, she saw her mother in prayer making it her first introduction to Christ's salvation. Even though she didn't understand it then, she developed her own personal relationship with her Lord and Savior.

It is with great honor for her to write about a woman who played a significant role in molding her into the woman she is today. Katie Lee Boyd Richardson, is she who sacrificed.

For more information about, Betty R. Smith please email brs0011@gmail.com.

A MOTHER'S HEART VOLUME 3 - CHAPTER 8

Betty R. Smith

A Mother's Heart
is Everything

Proverbs 31:10

"Strength and honour are her clothing; and she shall rejoice in time to come."

Chapter 9

A Warrior Woman like Deborah
Dr. Evelyn Bethune: A Legacy of Strength, Faith, and Redemption

By Elizabeth Bethune and Marcia Johnson

Judges 4: 4-7

4 *Now Deborah, a prophet, the wife of Lappidoth, was*
leading Israel at that time. ***5*** *She held court under the*
Palm of Deborah between Ramah and Bethel in the hill
country of Ephraim, and the Israelites went up to her to
have their disputes decided. ***6*** *She sent for Barak son of*
Abinoam from from Kedesh in Naphtali and said to him,

"The Lord, the God of Israel, commands you: 'Go, take with you ten thousand men of Naphtali and Zebulun and lead them up to Mount Tabor. 7 I will lead Sisera, the commander of Jabin's army, with his chariots and his troops to the Kishon River and give him into your hands.'"

To our beloved mother, Dr. Evelyn Bethune—

As your daughters, Elizabeth Bethune and Marcia Johnson, we are honored to celebrate you—not just as our mother, but as a woman of extraordinary strength, wisdom, and faith. You are a testament to resilience, a woman who has not only carried the legacy of our great-grandmother, Dr. Mary McLeod Bethune, but has also forged your own path, inspiring countless others along the way. Your story is one of triumph, not because your journey has been free of hardship, but because you have faced adversity with courage and emerged stronger each time.

A Legacy of Powerful Women

You are the granddaughter of Dr. Mary McLeod Bethune, a woman whose vision and leadership transformed the lives of so many. But before you were a leader in your own right, you were a daughter, learning from another extraordinary woman—our grandmother, Elizabeth (Beth) Bethune. Through her, you inherited the grace and determination that have defined your life's work.

Grandma Beth was a woman of quiet strength, a guiding force in your life who instilled in you the values of perseverance, humility, and service. You are carrying forth the lessons of strong Black women in your life, including that of your grandmother, Dr. Mary McLeod Bethune. Because of her, you learned early on that leadership is not about seeking power but about serving others. You learned that integrity is not about perfection but about owning your truth, standing firm in your faith, and continually striving to do better. You have carried those lessons with you, and they have shaped the woman you are today.

Strength in the Face of Adversity

Dr. Mary McLeod Bethune once said, "*The true worth of a race must be measured by the character of its womanhood.*"

If ever there were a woman who exemplifies character, courage, and perseverance, it is you.

Life has not always been easy, and you have made your share of mistakes—some that brought your judgment into question, some that tested your relationships, and some that could have broken a lesser woman. But you refused to let your past define you. Instead, you faced every challenge head-on, never shying away from the difficult work of healing, growing, and regaining the trust of those around you. You never gave up on your mission, and because of that, your faith in God only grew stronger.

Your ability to rebuild and restore has become one of your greatest strengths. You understand the weight of redemption because you have lived it. You know what it means to fall and rise again, to be broken and restored. That is why you lead with compassion, why you fight for truth and justice, and why you have dedicated your life to empowering others. You do not simply teach lessons—you live them. Your life is a living testimony to the power of faith, resilience, and the unwavering grace of God.

A Teacher, A Leader, A Warrior

Dr. Mary McLeod Bethune also said, "Whatever glory belongs to the race for a development unprecedented in history for the given length of time, a full share belongs to the womanhood of the race." You have carried that truth in everything you do. Your work with History in the Making Coaching Network, your commitment to uplifting Black women, and your relentless pursuit of justice all speak to your belief that women—especially Black women—deserve to be seen, heard, and valued.

But what makes you an even more powerful leader is that you do not just speak from a place of success; you speak from experience. You know what it means to struggle, to question yourself, to walk through fire. And because you have endured, you are able to guide others with honesty and authenticity. You do not just inspire people—you show them, through your own life, that restoration is possible, that faith is transformative, and that purpose is always within reach.

A Mother's Love, A Family's Strength

As your daughters, we have been blessed to witness your journey up close. We have seen the depth of your love, the fire of your determination, and the unshakable faith that guides your path. You have been our greatest teacher, showing us what it means to walk in truth, to own our past without shame, and to use every experience—good or bad—as a stepping stone to greater wisdom.

You have taught us that leadership is not about being flawless but about being fearless. That power is not about control but about the ability to lift others up. That faith is not just something we speak about but something we live. Because of you, we know that strength is not the absence of struggle—it is the willingness to keep going, no matter what.

The Power of Redemption and Faith

Your life is proof that redemption is real, that mistakes do not have to define us, and that God's grace is always available to those who seek it. You have never hidden from your past, and because of that, you have been able to help others find their own path to healing. Your transparency, your honesty, and your refusal to give up have given countless women the courage to reclaim their lives.

You are more than a mother. You are a movement. A force of nature. A living testament to the legacy of Dr. Mary McLeod Bethune and Elizabeth Flossie Bethune. Your work will continue to inspire generations to come, just as your grandmother and mother inspired you.

Dr. Evelyn Bethune, you are a warrior. A survivor. A teacher. A beacon of hope. You have turned your trials into testimonies, your failures into fuel, and your setbacks into stepping stones for others to follow. We honor you, we celebrate you, and we thank you for your relentless love, your unwavering example, and your fearless pursuit of truth.

With all our love and admiration,

Elizabeth V. Bethune & Marcia Johnson

A Mother's Heart is Everything

Dr. Evelyn Bethune

A Mother's Heart is Everything

Chapter 10

A Mother's Prayers Never Expire

By Theresa Jordan

I am grateful for the steadfast prayers of my mother, Eloise Wade, which continue to be answered today. Though I can't remember the exact timeframe, I remember her giving me six of her composition books, where she dedicated her time and prayers to the Lord every day. She would repeatedly begin her letters with, "Good morning, my Lord Jesus."

Within these notebooks, I could find prayers about her grandchildren, including twins Richard and Katherine, who were in the intensive care unit as premature babies in 2020. The doctors felt they were encountering a hopeless situation. However, my mother fervently interceded on their behalf, and I am grateful to say, "The Lord heard her prayers."

My mother had unwavering faith, and she knew Jesus was faithful and He was a promise keeper. She would consistently praise the Lord, and the following songs are constant reminders of my mother: "Praise is What I Do," by William Murphy and "Every Praise," by Bishop Hezekiah Walker.

My mother had such a forgiving heart, knowing it was important to forgive others if she wanted the Lord to forgive her. She recognized the Lord as her Jehovah Jireh, which meant her provider. Deep down, she knew no matter what challenges she encountered in life, Jesus was the best problem solver, and there was nothing too hard for God.

Her notebooks had numerous pages expressing her gratitude to the Lord for her children, grandchildren, and family. She would ask the Lord to surround them with His guardian angels during the day and night, and even throughout their lives. My mother knew for herself that "God was good all the time, and all the time God is good."

Because she had a personal relationship with Him for herself, she knew firsthand what the Lord could do. She reminded me of Psalm 121, which states, "I will lift up mine eyes unto the hills, from whence cometh my help." She understood that all her help came from the Lord.

Every day, she intentionally took the time to express the matters of heart. Proverbs 4:23 says, "Keep thy heart with diligence; for out of it are the issues of life."

Throughout her journey, my mother knew Jesus would never leave or forsake her. If she stumbled, she knew the Lord would pick her back up. Even when she experienced difficult times, she trusted Jesus because He was the greatest problem solver. Jesus has the best resolutions. He was also the One responsible for being the lifter of her head. He could also turn her weeping into dancing, and if she held out the Lord would fight her battles.

My mother often recognized that the Lord treated her better than she could have treated herself. She understood that she couldn't fix everything on her own, but the Lord had the power and ability to fix all things.

Jesus brought her the greatest joy, and this joy the world didn't give and couldn't take it away. She knew that nobody could do her like Jesus. He was responsible for turning her tears into laughter and knew how to bring a smile to her face.

She knew this world was not our permanent home, and everyone had an appointed time to leave this earth. My mother often remarked, "We have one foot out and the other foot in the grave." She understood that we had a choice about where our permanent home would be for eternity, and we were just passing through. This serves as a powerful reminder to be intentional in our actions for the Lord and others.

This reminds me of the scripture, "So teach us to number our days, that we may apply our hearts unto wisdom" found in Psalm 90:12. Whenever she faced problems, she believed in God's word about adversity, which encouraged her to "Be still, and she would see the salvation of the

Lord." My mother acknowledged that Jesus was greater than the problems she or her family would face in life.

My mom never focused on material things; Jesus' love was sufficient for her. Throughout my mother's notebooks, she expressed nothing but gratitude to the Lord for her guardian angels, and she thanked her angels for watching over her both day and night. My mother's favorite scripture was Psalm 91, which reminded her of God's overall protection over herself and our family.

She recognized Jesus as being a mind regulator, and He was responsible for giving her strength and good health. My mother understood she was blessed and knew her blessings came from the Lord.

She was an extraordinary woman of faith. I can remember when the Lord blessed me with Triumphant Magazine Publishing, and I encountered a woman who had her own magazine. This remarkable lady became my mentor, and her services were not free, I dedicated six months to her mentorship program. Ultimately, I had to make an executive decision to begin doing things on my own. I can still remember my mother encouraging me, saying, "Baby, you got this, and you will begin doing greater things than your mentor."

At the time, I had difficulty seeing the same vision my mother had for me, but I chose to trust her words for my life. My writing experience was limited, and to be honest, I was lost in the process. I will never forget that Bartee and Angie BEE were scheduled to be featured in April 2017. My mother spoke life into my dreams, and she believed God would perform the impossible in my life.

And guess what? The Lord honored our requests and this October 2025 marks eight remarkable years - truly thriving and flourishing for the Lord.

When I visited my mother's house after the Lord called her home on November 4, 2019, I discovered copies of all the Triumphant Magazine in cabinets, drawings, and various places. Thank you, Mom for your consistent prayers and unwavering faith. God heard and answered our prayers. She never mentioned what I couldn't achieve; instead, she encouraged and inspired me to reach the impossible. My mother's words were powerful, and she chose to speak life over me.

She truly believed in Jesus' words about having faith the size of a mustard seed and believed we have not because we ask not. I'm grateful that my mother's prayers will never expire. Mom, I truly appreciate how your prayers continue to move mountains in our lives. Thank you, Jesus, for blessing me with a praying mother.

A Mother's Heart is Everything

My Mother, Eloise Wade.

Greater Things are Coming in June 2025

A Father's HEART

VOLUME 1

FEATURING 8 PHENOMENAL AUTHORS

THERESA JORDAN - VISIONARY

Theresa Jordan

Thank you for choosing

A Mother's Heart

Anthology Volume 3

www.ingramcontent.com/pod-product-compliance
Lightning Source LLC
Chambersburg PA
CBHW070626310726
48982CB00001B/180

9798990403512